FEB 2 8 2021

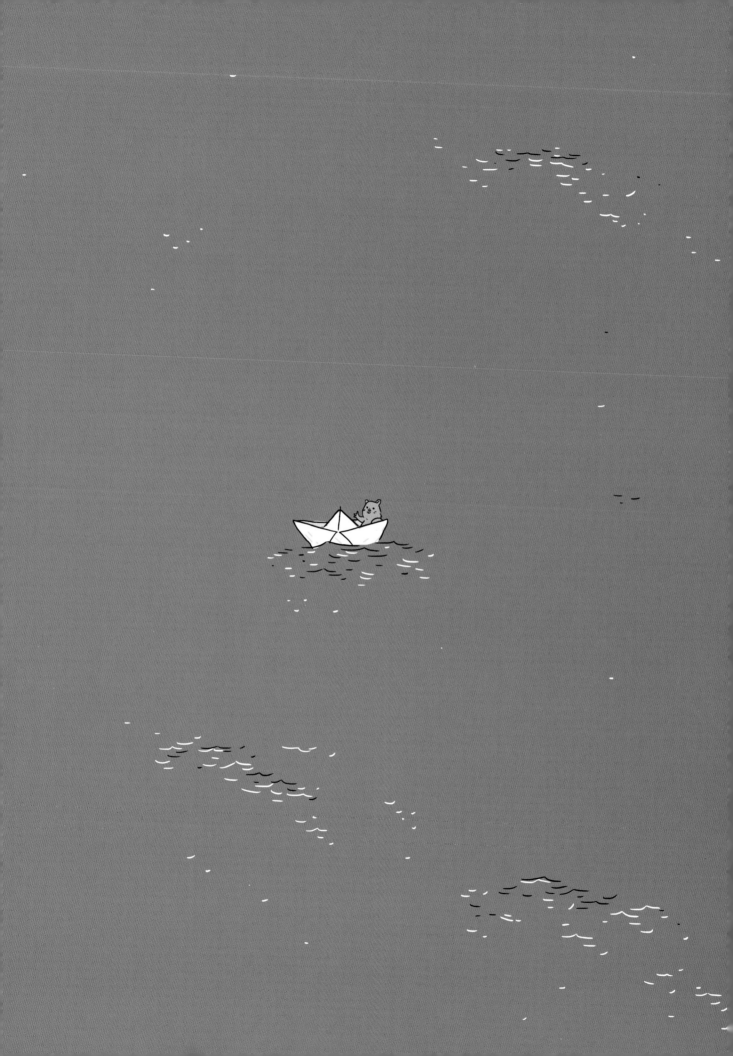

For my Ruth & Shachar

English translation rights arranged through S.B. Rights Agency – Stephanie Barrouillet

First U.S. edition 2020

Library of Congress Catalog Card Number pending
ISBN 978-1-5362-1143-6

LEO 25 24 23 22 21 20
10 9 8 7 6 5 4 3 2 1

Printed in Heshan, Guangdong, China

This book was typeset in LiebeRuth.
The illustrations were created digitally.

Candlewick Press
99 Dover Street
Somerville, Massachusetts 02144

visit us at www.candlewick.com

SANDCASTLE

Einat Tsarfati

CANDLEWICK PRESS

I love building castles in the sand.
So I built a sandcastle.

But not just any castle.

A real castle, with domes and turrets
and a crocodile moat.

And large windows
with an ocean view.

It was not long before kings and queens from all over the world came to visit my castle.

"It's one hundred percent sand," murmured a king with a curly mustache.

"And you can hear the ocean!" added a queen with a fancy pearl necklace.

They were very impressed.
Especially with the dining hall,
which served ice cream around the
clock — any kind, any time.

That evening, we held a grand party in the ballroom.
Dollops of ice cream were served all night long.
It was awesome.

"Yuck! The royal almond strudel is full
of sand!" one king shouted.

"All this sand makes my tongue feel like a
beached jellyfish!" complained a queen as she
laid down her napkin.

The next day, the Triathlon of Knights Tournament was
completely ruined.

"Aargh! There is sand in my suit of armor!" sobbed the bravest
knight in the kingdom. "I can't even lift a card from the pile."

In the glorious greenhouse, all the rare plants wilted. They do not grow very well in sand (except for the cacti, which felt right at home).

"There are grains of sand in between my royal toes. It is so itchy," muttered a queen.

"It is highway robbery," grumbled a king who could not open his royal treasure chests because the locks were full of sand.

"This is unacceptable,"
roared a king whose daily fig milk bath
was utterly spoiled by sand.

"I'll never be able to fall asleep like this," snapped an old queen
as she tried to shake the sand out of her Egyptian cotton sheets.
"It's even worse than a single pea underneath my mattress."

Everyone was so angry!

I didn't know what to do. My whole castle was made of sand.

That's how it is with sandcastles.

So I made a sand ball. . . .

Guests in dresses and robes and suits of armor and towels and pajamas all took aim. . . .

Three brave queens joined forces on the balcony.

Two kings made a pact to take control of the staircase.

Suddenly...

in came the sea and washed everything away.

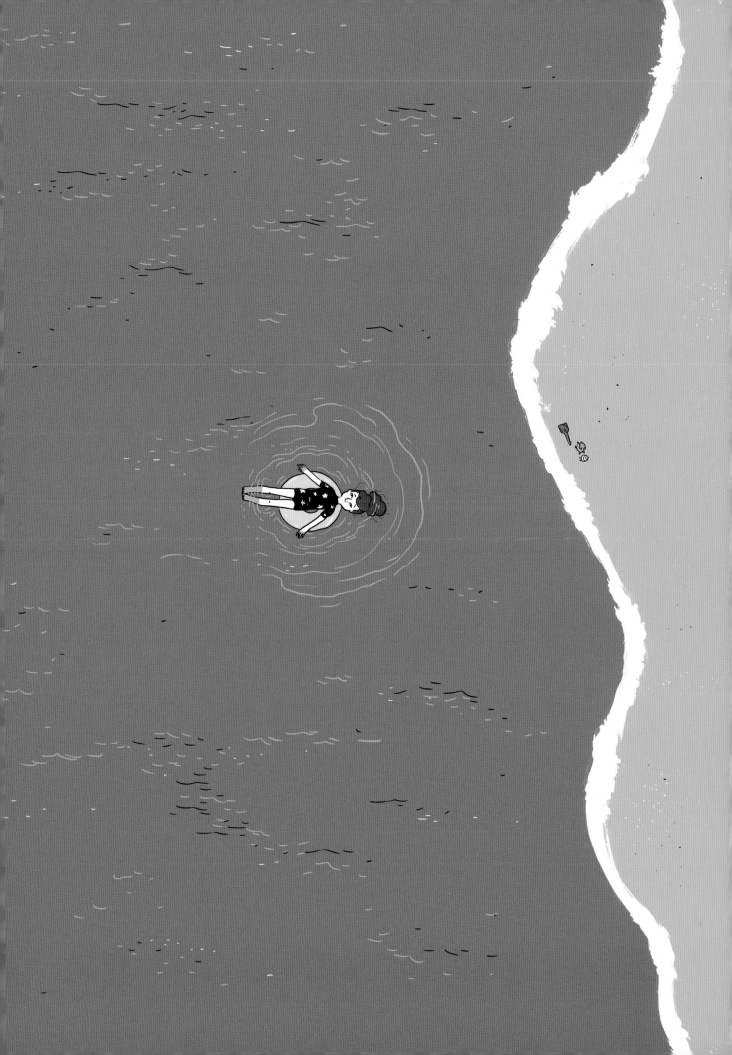

So I built a sandcastle.

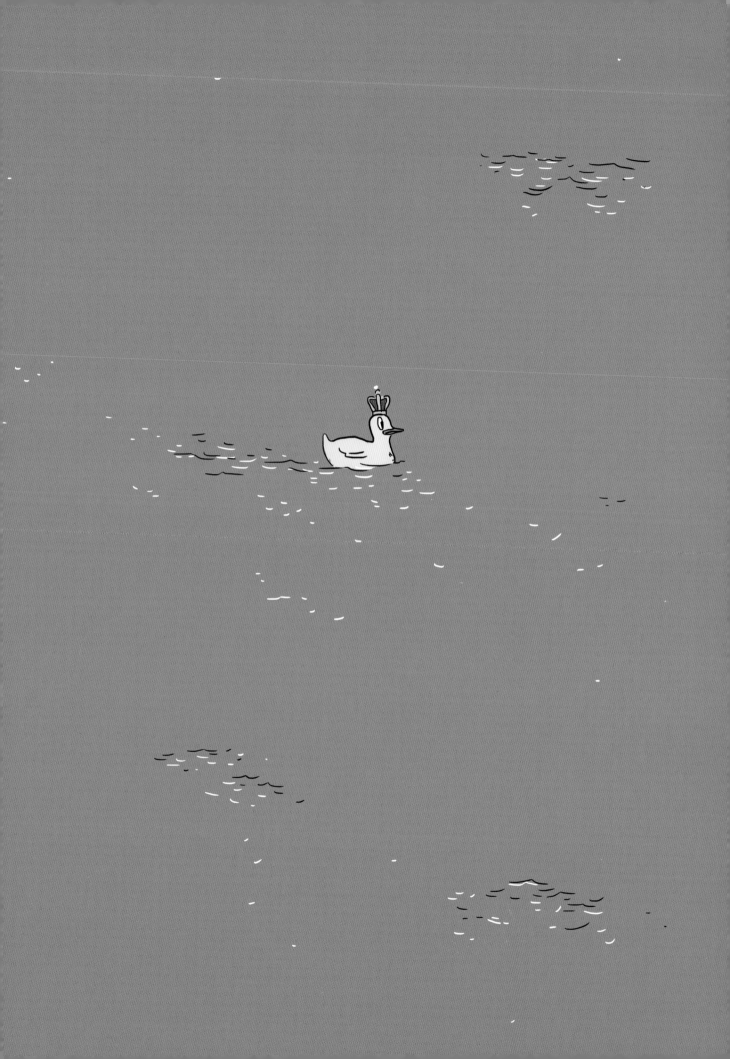